T0063290

MetaMorphosis

MetaMorphosiS

Legends Come to Life . . .

Sankalpita Mullick

PARTRIDGE

ISBN: Softcover   978-1-4828-8454-8
               eBook   978-1-4828-8453-1

To order additional copies of this book, contact
Partridge India
000 800 10062 62
orders.india@partridgepublishing.com

www.partridgepublishing.com/india

Index (read at your own risk):

Dedication

I would like to dedicate this book to my parents-
Dr. Paramita Mukherjee Mullick and Mr. Sudip Mullick
and the cutest pet ever, Harry.

ACKNOWLEDGEMENT

I would like to thank so many people that reader, you should get a tub of popcorn and some coffee to keep you company. This is going to be long. I would first and foremost thank my parents for helping me with my book and my pet for not screaming his head off while I was writing my book. I cannot thank Partridge enough for helping me accomplish this feat. I thank my wonderful grandparents and a fistful of true friends that I have. I would like to thank you-the reader for taking some time out and reading my book and (hopefully) enjoying it. Last but not the least; I thank my teachers without whom school wouldn't be half as fun.

THANK YOU ALL!!

PREFACE

I had always wondered what had happened to the villains after the battle. The heroes got their happily ever after but the villains who had actually put in similar effort in the fight were left to rot. Two people fighting each other can never be that different. They just believe in different things. I thought it to be unfair that they weren't given a second chance because at the end of the day they did not lose because they were entirely bad but because they had that one bad trait which led to their downfall. Be it pride, obsession, insecurity or hate, they too had a life before it was uprooted and made into pulp. So I sincerely hope you enjoy this story about villains, enemies and hate which teach us about heroes, friendship and love.

Over and out,

Sankalpita Mullick.

FOREWORD

I have seen my daughter Sankalpita Mullick bloom from a tiny bud to a beautiful flower. Not only does her charming smile make her attractive but also her intelligence, her clarity of thought and compassionate nature make her a wonderful teenager. Pebble, as I lovingly call her, astonished me one day when she told me she was writing a novel. After reading the manuscript I was overwhelmed to see the maturity in a fourteen year old girl. At this tender age she feels a villain in the mythological stories also needs a second chance. We adults condemn such villains as losers whereas she, a young teenager feels that they too have their good qualities. I am happy to introduce this book to you which changed my perception of the word 'villain'.

Dr. Paramita Mukherjee Mullick

August 15, 2016

The Bombshell

"Would you like to know your future?
If your answer is yes, think again. Not knowing is
the greatest life motivator.
So enjoy, endure, survive, each moment as it
comes to you in its proper sequence -- a surprise."

– Vera Nazarian,
The Perpetual Calendar of Inspiratio

I pressed the enter button on my new search. I had typed 'Metamorphosis' in the search engine and was now staring at a new page with bloodshot eyes. This new tab had a picture of a magnificent black building standing amidst a clearing surrounded by vast forested lands. The only question that was nagging me at the back of my mind was that, "What was I doing at 3 am on a Monday, searching some boring school in the Andaman and Nicobar Islands?" Answering this question was hard because I was being dragged away from my family, from my friends, from my school and the beautiful, life-of-party attitude of Mumbai because of some…..test? Apparently some school in the Andaman and Nicobar Islands thought I was good enough to be one of their students out of 2000 students in my school. I had my doubts about this extremely …life changing (read as: stupid) journey. It all started with that 'aptitude test'. I wish someone would have told me that the winner would be selected to attend the most elite school in Southern-Asia. My parents were thrilled but I was not because I had seen the uniform or rather the shapeless sack we had to wear (at the assembly, at least!) every day which looked like it was made by a five year old. We had to tie our hair in two plaits …as if one wasn't enough (I thank my stars for getting a shorter haircut…I bless the summer heat in Mumbai!). The structure too was fully black and looked like the devil's fun house. I was too shocked in the morning to react when that e-mail came. It was like a black cat had eaten a cracked mirror on Friday the thirteenth while a crow cawed, bringing bad luck with it wherever it went. They informed us about my selection as a student in their school. It wasn't a very old school I think only 2 years old but it was hard, very hard to get an admission in it. Worse than even the rag-like uniforms and stringent rules was the name. I mean really, 'Metamorphosis'. I don't want to go to a school where the name means 'a change of the form or nature of a thing or person into a completely different one'*. Just then I heard the sound of footsteps climbing the flight of steps which instantly alerted me. Anyone who saw me after this would have no idea I was surfing the net. I slept snoring loudly, for an outsider to make sure that I was asleep. If you call sleeping -shaking with rage and anxiety about an irritating trip in a semi-lighted room with a laptop screen blaring in your face with one eye open. Now I could only wait for my vexing voyage to Ross Island....

(*It is entirely up to you what you would want to interpret 'Metamorphosis' as, this is strictly the scientific definition.)

IDEA BANK - Draw, paint, doodle or write what you liked/disliked in this book. Leave notes for your friends or simply finish that maths sum you have been avoiding

Some Facts on Ross Island

Why Ross Island? Obviously it is the coolest Island on the planet and that is the reason I have made it the prime location in this tale. Those of you readers who assumed the above lines to be true are wrong. Ross Island is not cool but quaint, pretty, nice, cute and sweet so basically I choose something relatable. Sweetness over popularity any day. Ross Island is one of the Andaman and Nicobar Islands, about 2 km east of Port Blair. It was the Administrative Headquarters for the islands (cool right, but unfortunately...well read on), before an earthquake rocked it in 1941. The headquarters was then shifted to Port Blair. One can see remnants of an opulent past in the ruins of the church, swimming pool and the Chief Commissioner's residence with its huge gardens and grand ballrooms. There is also a cemetery and a small museum managed by the Indian Navy. The museum has on display a collection of old records.

Ross Island can be reached by a short boat ride from Water Sports Complex. The island is controlled by the Indian Navy, which requires every visitor to sign in on entering.

The small island with its treasure of ruins in it became the hot tourist spot in the territory. People desire to know more and more about Ross Island. This Island, is a tiny island situated a few kilometres away from Port Blair city. The island presently houses the ruins of old buildings like the state Ballroom, the Chief Commissioner's House, the Government House, Church, the old 'Andamanese Home', Hospital, Bakery, Press, Swimming Pool and Troop Barracks, all in dilapidated condition, reminiscent of the old British regime. Ever since Dr. James Pattison Walker arrived in Port Blair aboard the East India Company's steam frigate 'Senuramis' on 10 March 1858, this island remained under British occupation till 1942. From 1942 to 1945, the island was under the occupation of Japan. However, the allies reoccupied the island in 1945 and later abandoned it. During British occupation, this island was the seat of power of the British.

In November 1857, the Government decided to establish a penal settlement in Andaman and send "hard-core elements" among those who took on the British. There were two reasons: One, to keep them away from other prisoners and the other, to send out a message that a similar treatment would be meted out to anyone who challenged the British authority.

IDEA BANK - Draw, paint, doodle or write what you liked/disliked in this book. Leave notes for your friends or simply finish that maths sum you have been avoiding

"Pragyaaaa!"

The Vexing Voyage

"It is like a voyage of discovery into unknown lands, seeking not for new territory but for new knowledge. It should appeal to those with a good sense of adventure."

– Frederick Sanger

The next day I heard the uncannily familiar shouts of, 'Pragya' at 6 in the morning. I was as sleepy as Kumbhakarna*. Maybe it was the being awake till 3. Maybe. My bag was neatly packed with the delicate material on the top and the rough and the hard at the bottom. It looked like it was packed by the neatest person in the world. Yes it was, because it was packed by the neatest person, my mom. She was the one who was calling me down for breakfast. I hadn't checked my phone from like a long time, so when I unlocked it, it showed a freaking 256 messages! All my friends wishing me good luck and farewell, not that I didn't need it, I knew it was going to be awful anyway. So I boarded the loooooo oooooooooooooooooooooooooong plane ride and ordered

5 cups of soft drinks just to calm my nerves. I am afraid it did the opposite. So now I am dreaming of my new school, and yeah I am not sleeping (tip: don't try watching dreams while awake, it hardly ever happens). The flight finally lands at Port Blair where we take a boat to Ross Island. My parents are supposed to drop me at the entrance of the school where the principal will call all the new arrivals. The rules said that we had to enter in our school uniform, which I am wearing right now and looking like a complete dork. To top it all, my hair looks like it has soaked buckets and buckets of oil. This actually is the horrifying truth because without buckets of oil my frizzy hair could never be made into a hairstyle which at least resembles a normal one. The boat ride was bumpy and the students' faces were blurred so I could see only their uniforms. It was more of a yacht than a boat, the schools private yacht for the students to come from Port Blair to Ross Island. The yacht ride was pretty long and I can't say I exactly hit it off with the person next to me. We couldn't sit with our parents because apparently we had to 'interact' and 'get to know our fellow students'. They wish. I could see what I will be suffering for the next few years, right next to me. A total airhead and snob was sitting next to me with 'I don't really care' written all over her face. She easily might be in a class ahead of me, but that obviously didn't give her the right to look at me with disgust. When I was like, "Hi, there", she was like, "Whateves". I just gave her a bemused smirk. Or at least I meant to. My smirks often come out as ugly scowls. I had accepted the fact that I would be an outcast. But no one, no one, and especially not this thinking-herself-to-be-great person would outright insult me. I wouldn't let them. Being likeable was my trademark.

But this was a scenario where only fittest (or rather meanest) survived. So now I was in a strangish place with the weirdest people. This was going to be fun.

*A character in the epic Ramayana who slept for 6 months in a year and ate the rest of the time. Lucky guy!

IDEA BANK - Draw, paint, doodle or write what you liked/disliked in this book. Leave notes for your friends or simply finish that maths sum you have been avoiding

The School

"I hope you're pleased with yourselves. We could all have been killed - or worse, expelled. Now if you don't mind, I'm going to bed."

– J.K. Rowling,
Harry Potter and the Sorcerer's Stone

You could say the school was wonderful, royal and well-funded but I only found one word, "Magnificent". I heard a voice which I would now recognise even in hell and it said one word which made me laugh like crazy, "Whateves". It was the same girl who sat with me on the yacht, her name was Ragini (as read her gold plated name tag). She had used that word for the fifteenth time in 2 hours. That had to be some kind of a record. She glared at me with piercing, jet black eyes and said some unspeakable words under her breath but loud enough for me to hear. So, I did the obvious thing, I glared back. My mom and dad had already left with lots of hugs and kisses to and from both. Finally a school representative came and took us inside. We entered the school at sunset, when it looked more like a haunted palace than a school. We were going to the principal's office where she would have a word with us. All I could see were winding staircases, intricate archways, glowing chandeliers and inscripted stone pillars. All the inscriptions were in Hindi and Sanskrit. But one stood out: वयम् वितर्कयति अन्तः क्षण अवसर.

Without realising I spoke out, "We believe in second chances..." The guide looked back like I had severely offended him. With a volume tapering with every word he said, "That's what is written...it is the school motto... how did you...what...you know ...how?!" Though shocked at his sudden interest in me after deciphering an ancient language* I quickly managed it by telling the group how I had learned the school guidebook by heart which seemed to calm everyone's racing pulse. Wow, this school is so much weirder then I had expected. Also pretty orthodox because they were all about keeping away evil and the Lord protecting the school. I suddenly bumped into something. It was a fountain. This was ridiculous. A fountain in the middle of the school! On asking the guard he pointed at heaps of coins at the bottom, which I had surprisingly failed to notice. He said, "This is a wishing well. It is said that someone whose heart is pure, if at a moment of weakness and need, throws a coin in it...their wish will come true". And making that extraordinary comment he resumed his composed manner, which, had wavered for a moment (again!). I stared at him like he had just predicted the future or something. Then snapping out of it I ran after the group. *Sanskrit

Irksome Introductions

A real friend is one who walks in when rest of the
world walks out.

– Walter Winchell

We were now waiting very im-patiently outside the
principal's office for what was to come. Everyone had a
kind of nervous tension waiting to break free in them,
except Ragini. Well, I didn't bother about her because I
have stopped including her in the human category. There
were two big oak doors, two ferocious looking guards and
a cute swan blocking our entrance. I have never seen such
a beautiful swan. One of the guards was carrying it. On
asking he told me that it was the headmistress' pet. Finally
we were ushered in. The truth…it was not what I expected.
There were books; trophies and medals like there should be
in a principal's office. But, there was also an electric guitar,
keyboard, iPods, iPads, some hundred-thousand laptops, a
gazillion books and one main state- of -the–art computer. It
was as if someone went to an electronic sale with the budget

being unlimited (and hogged on the book sale next to it!). Did I mention there was also a mini robot walking on the desk and an automatic cup holder which crushes the cup after use? Behind the mini robot was a dignified, beautiful looking woman who wasn't so dignified and beautiful in her current situation. She was bending over the robot with soot and oil on her face and muttering to herself, and basically not noticing us. Then the guide spoke up, "Dr.S…". The woman looked up and gave us a welcoming smile. She wiped the soot of her face and told us to sit down. There were only new admissions in the room, the old ones were already sent up to their dormitories. "Welcome, to Metamorphosis. Our aim here is to turn you all into new human beings and I really hope for a better not for a worse result." Then Miss S. added, "That was what the school wants me to say. I just want to say follow your heart and brain, you, will emerge successful. And now…..the introductions." She started scribbling in a small notebook. There was one Nandini, two Shreyas one Rahul and three Alis. When I told my name she looked up, and then went back to writing the names. Lastly she said, "Don't go about doing any mischief", and she winked at me. There was a strange feeling in the pit of my stomach but I ignored it and exited. Strange, very strange…..

On checking the list of dormitories I saw that I was sharing one with the girl named Nandini (same shivering person standing next to me in Dr.S' office). So now that we are roomies I went out searching for her.

Making Best Friends
and Worst Enemies

Your best friend and worst enemy are both in this
room right now. It's not your neighbour right or
left - and it's not God or the devil - it's you.

– Edwin Louis Cole

Oh.My.God.The Principal's office. The one place my
principle's would never allow me to go...at least not for
something like this. I had come here because my stupid and
defiant heart had betrayed my sensible brain.

Flashback

I was frantically searching for Nandini in my desperate
attempt to make friends in this unthinkably cold and
hostile territory. Finally I came to the cafeteria which was
pretty full. On asking someone, I realised that some poor
soul was being ragged.....something which is increasing
day by day. I never quite grasped the concept of one

human making another their own physical or mental punching bag. I was always against this form of so called 'entertainment' and went forward to see if I could help the poor victim. It was Nandini. She was stammering incoherently, something about being sorry for what she had done. I caught the words that could be heard through her whimpering like a puppy with his leg stuck under a heavy pole. "S….s…sorr…y…Ra…gi…ni" she said. That was the moment when I fully acknowledged the presence of the other girl in the centre of the crowd. With almond shaped eyes a sharp nose and cruel, cold eyes you could just imagine her playing the wicked witch or evil stepsister/mother in a story (oh, and did I mention she was also the charming young lady with black eyes on the yacht…did I say charming? I meant a grade A pain in the posterior). She was fuming and if you looked closely and had a wild imagination you could see smoke coming out of her ears and nostrils. Without hearing her speak or even do anything at all I could tell that she was the 'queen bee' of this school. She was shaken out of her stupor and stopped giving Nandini the evil eye because she had a new target …me. I had stooped down to pick up Nandini's bag and then tugged at her arm. She just stared at me stupefied. Finally she budged. While walking away with Nandini looking at me like I was a Martian's sister someone tugged at Nandini's bag which caused me to (well in a nursery rhyme way …) have a great fall. I was not amused. I knew just too well who had done it but ***as if*** by reflex I kicked that person hard. The joke's not on me now, is it? Ragini was plain, pathetically shocked.

End of Flashback

So basically that is the reason I was standing outside the principal's office staring at the board with 'Principal' written on it whilst I awaited my punishment.

IDEA BANK - Draw, paint, doodle or write what you liked/disliked in this book. Leave notes for your friends or simply finish that maths sum you have been avoiding

Royal Rooms

Service is the rent that you pay for room on this
earth.

– Shirley Chisholm

She looked disappointed. The last expression I imagined her to have after creating havoc on the first day at school. I mean where was the shock, the anger? It was almost as if she dealt with extraordinarily mischievous children every day. Or maybe she did…Okay I am forgetting the main topic out here. Me. Well me and Ragini but it feels nice to include only yourself in a topic. I forced my brain to listen to what Dr.S was saying, "…especially of you, Pragya". Wait what? I had spaced out of the conversation thinking about the punishment that she might give me, hearing my name I suddenly blurted out, "Um, Sorry".

"Focus", said Dr.S, "Your tests are in a month you two are better of studying and I am sure it will look better on your record if you score well in your tests rather than attacking your friends". She then dismissed us. If looks could kill, my funeral procession would be on the go right now, judging by the glare Ragini was sending my way. Yeah right as if it weren't her fault too. I gave her a 'see-if-I-care-look' and walked away to find my room.

Oh.My.God. Pinch me someone. After climbing winding staircases and crossing dark and mysterious hallways I had finally found my room. Room number 108. It was lavender. At least half of it was lavender with splashes of white and the other side light pink with a greyish tinge and grey accessories while my side had white accessories. Yes my side. I knew immediately that the lavender and white side was mine, it was my favourite colour(s) after all. I loved it was an understatement. I saw Nandini's bag in the pink and grey side which was separated from my side by a beautiful turquoise blue curtain. The bed was fluffier and softer than my favourite teddy. Everything was perfect. Too perfect in fact!

The Teachers Guide

Education is the key to success in life,
and teachers make a lasting impact
in the lives of their students.

– Solomon Ortiz

The teachers. Surprisingly we hadn't met even one of them expect Dr.S. Obviously if they have to teach us they have to meet us at some point of time. A huge-I mean refrigerator huge-blackboard greeted us when we were assembled in the auditorium. It was a large spacious room with something indisputably cold lurking behind the walls. Walls which were covered with cheerful posters. The blackboard had names written and subjects written next to them. It looked like this:

1. Mr.Avran-Language and Literature
2. Mr.Shkad -Hindi
3. Miss.Kaholi-History
4. Miss.Sukarphana-Geography

5. Miss.Rathmana-Current Affairs
6. Mrs.Keikaiy-Etiquette
7. Mr.Dyuordhan-Physical Education
8. Mr.Akushin-Indoor Sports
9. Mr.Sanak-Science
10. Mr.Karnabhakum-Mathematics

After reading the list I seriously didn't know if I was more bemused or seriously shocked. Were we not going to meet the teachers yet...what sort of names were these?...Now what? There was no co-ordinator or any kind of authoritative figure around. All these questions were racing in my mind when the totally unexpected happened. Okay, not ninja turtle or poisonous cobras, but close. The lights went off. The huge number of students who weren't exactly quiet and calm with the lights on was now running helter-skelter. It was a stampede for God's sake. I felt someone push me but honestly didn't care because I was doing the same to countless nameless and faceless people (literally, because it was pitch dark). Then suddenly the lights were switched on and there were ten figures standing on the stage. Eleven if you count Dr.S. They were teachers. They gave out that authoritative and 'I will **_not_** tolerate it' vibe.

I scrutinised them carefully, while they were delivering their speeches starting from the left. The first was a robust man with a long moustache, stubble and an intelligent look in his eyes (which were hidden behind I-am-the-boss kind of smart spectacles) but an arrogant stride. I caught the last words of his speech, "…and facing challenges is making the difference, thank you". He was our literature and language teacher Avran.

The second was Mr Shkad. He was not too puny but also not very well-built. To be truthful, he looked like a very emotional person. He tried to remain modest but some faded aristocracy shone on him. He finished his speech with the word, "…never think you are wiser or smarter than your elders because then the joke is on you".

Next was Miss. Kaholi. She certainly had a fiery personality. I had a feeling her kindest punishment included a visit to the hospital. She had a croaky voice and a fairly simple get up, with no makeup which highlighted her natural beauty. The only thing her face lacked was a smile because she chose to adorn her face with a constant frown. She ended with, "… learn the fire safety rules and never play unfair". I personally like the first one better. More practical.

Oh.My.God.The next teacher looked just like the woman who used to pull my cheeks at weddings or the boy who used to throw my pencil down the drain. She basically looked like that someone who does some petty crime which actually leaves a big impact on your life. Not to mention she looked like *the* gossip girl. She looked more like a person who likes Bollywood gossip more than the tiny things in life like who is the prime minister of a country or the stock market news. She wasn't audible, even with a microphone. So I have no idea what she said. I have no clue what Miss. Rathmana is going to teach.

The next teacher was such a contrast to Miss. Rathmana that I think my eyes had some trouble focusing. She was gorgeous, drop-dead gorgeous. I have no clue if she is or ever was beautiful because her face was hidden behind layers and layers and layers and……………layers of makeup. She was wearing a cocktail dress which kind of looked more like she was attending a party and her hair let down made up into perfect curls and with golden highlights complementing her fair face and wooden earrings, which would look awkward on other people but looked just too cute on her. Our etiquette teacher would be doing muuuch better in a fashion school. Trust me; she also had the **thickest** British accent which basically no one understood.

A well-built fellow graced the spot next to her. Anybody could guess he was the physical education teacher..... not only by his well-built body but also by his sporty outfit of track pants and a track suit. As if necessitated by his position he carried a basketball in his hand. Our school mascot was of all animals a …swan. At least they could have chosen a less graceful and peace loving creature. "Go swans go", was how Mr Dyuordhans speech ended. I murmured to the person next to me, "Shall we burst his bubble by telling him that swans are not the fastest of animals…and instead of 'Go Swans Go', he should try 'Slow Swans Slow'".

The fellow next to him looked old but had the mischievous glint of a young fellow in his eyes. To be precise he looked like a video gamer tired of finding cheat codes and shortcuts to pass just a level a.k.a all the levels. He introduced himself as our indoor sports teacher and concluded with, "…and always remember it is not strength which plays the winning turn but intelligence".

The next was an uninteresting man who was considerably well-built. He was Mr.Sanak. What caught my attention was, a peacock feather being crushed in his hand. Oh well, everyone has their own interests. He ended his short speech with, "Never trust anyone. Being self-independent is the key". Yeah, as if anyone cares.

The last teacher in the row wasn't a teacher. He was a giant..... 6 feet 10 inches approximately. A moustache invertly proportionate to his size that is as **huge** as he was, he owned a moustache equally small. It was, trust me laughable to the level infinity. He didn't say anything. Obviously because he was sleeping- like a little baby- and snoring, shaking his pot belly. He was considerably hilarious. I really trust mathematics class was going to be fun with Mr.Karnabhakum.

The madness of the teacher's introductions finished with someone throwing a litre of water on Mr.Karnabhakum. This day was going to be unforgettable.

IDEA BANK - Draw, paint, doodle or write what you liked/disliked in this book. Leave notes for your friends or simply finish that maths sum you have been avoiding

What Not To Do

You are remembered for the rules you break.

– Douglas MacArthur

Un-freaking-believable.

When we returned to our dorm rooms we saw a huge notice hanging outside our doors. It was long. It was weird. When I say weird, I mean cat-dragged-in crazy.

It was a to-do list. No scratch that, it was a <u>not</u> to do list. It looked something like this:

What not to do:

- No roaming around after 8pm.
- No abusing, teasing or insulting.
- No asking the teachers **anything** unrelated to the subject taught.
- No reading books (out of the syllabus) without a teacher's consent.

- No rumour about anyone to be spread or outright insult to be uttered.
- <u>Never</u> to venture in the staff room-without a teacher's consent.
- Phone call timings (to be followed strictly):5-6pm.
- No other language should be observed except for English (exception during the subject Hindi is being taught).
- No mimicry or making fun of the elders.
- No celebrating festivals while inside school premises.
- No asking your teacher for advice (if you want to do it at your own risk).

Signed: <u>*Dr. S*</u>

I had no idea what it meant but one thing was for sure. We, according to them had no life. We couldn't even enjoy at school, a boarding school that too. I was silently screaming nooooooooooooooooooooooooooooo……………..

After reading the meaningless parchment which we were supposed to follow strictly I went to take a shower. Now, I really loved the huge Jacuzzi which had refreshed flower petals (usually orchids-my favourite) spread over the lukewarm water. Nandini had a separate bathroom with roses instead of orchids. Understandably, her favourite flower. The worst part was the walls. They had pathetic sound proofing. This was the reason I could hear loud voices arguing. Normally I would not have eavesdropped but I heard my new-found foe Ragini's voice. "…WHO DOES SHE THINK SHE IS?!" I would love to know who could make Ragini so mad. Another voice was trying to calm her, "Its, alright…it was a long time ago…she did not know what she was doing…and this Pragya girl seems to be new…". Wait, what? They were talking about me? The second seemed to be a male voice. I was intrigued. I was curious. I know 'curiosity killed the cat', but I was smarter than a cat. I put a glass on the wall to help me hear better. Just then I had the ticklish sensation and sudden involuntary urge to sneeze…..."Aaaaaaa…choooo", I went startling myself. A grave mistake while snooping. I heard the boy's voice, "Who resides in the other room?" "Pragya…" answered Ragini. I was *so* dead.

IDEA BANK - Draw, paint, doodle or write what you liked/disliked in this book. Leave notes for your friends or simply finish that maths sum you have been avoiding

Boggling Books

"A room without books is like a body without a soul."

– Marcus Tullius Cicero

"The person, be it gentleman or lady,
who has not pleasure in a good novel,
must be intolerably stupid."

– Jane Austen

"Books are the quietest and most constant of friends;
they are the most accessible and wisest of counsellors,
and the most patient of teachers."

– Charles William Eliot

Books are (if you all have not yet realised) an essential part of school. I love books and rather pride myself on my ability to read, write and speak. Books have gotten me a far way and I think they were one of the most enriching and socially- helping inventions of mankind. In my opinion the only types of book, which makes absolutely no sense and thrives on our boredom are- textbooks. Evidently I am not the biggest fan of textbooks but then again I ***do not hate*** them nor am I easily puzzled by their writing. But this preposterous book list made me re-read it innumerable number of times. It looked something like this:

1. A BUNCH OF TABLOIDS.
2. SHAKESPEARE-SPECIAL EDITION OF COMEDIES ONLY.
3. ALL BOOKS ON ANCIENT WARFARE.
4. MAP OF INDIAN KINGDOMS.
5. HISTORY-NO BOOKS REQUIRED NOTES WILL BE GIVEN IN CLASS.
6. BOOKS ON VEDIC MATHEMATICS SHALL BE PROVIDED AND EXTRA REFERENCE BOOKS ARE ALLOWED.
7. 'WINNING –BY HOOK OR BY CROOK' AND 'INDOOR GAMING STRATEGIES'.
8. 'HOW TO BE A PRINCESS/PRINCE' AND 'THE VALUE OF ETIQUETTES'
9. 'BIG BANG THEORY-DID IT REALLY CREATE THE WORLD?' AND 'THE SCIENCE OF GODS'.
10. FOLKTALE BOOKS IN HINDI.

I had just escaped from the wrath of Ragini when I saw this list hanging on the wall outside Miss S' office. I was shocked but had that strange tingling feeling that this school has many more surprises planned…

IDEA BANK - Draw, paint, doodle or write what you liked/disliked in this book. Leave notes for your friends or simply finish that maths sum you have been avoiding

Creepy Classes

"Sometimes it's better to bunk a class and enjoy
with friends because today when I look back,
marks never made me laugh but memories do"

– APJ Abdul Kalam

The classes hit us like a shooting star, all of a sudden and out of the blue. With all the things happening we had completely forgotten our entire purpose of being there. We had actually forgotten the classes. Classes are important no doubt but at the same time incredibly boring. This was my opinion until the morning when the creepy classes started in my new school.

I was ready for a little peculiar but not for straight-out weird as I headed for my first class, current affairs…

If Miss. Rathmana's idea of an ideal class is a quiz on the who's who of Bollywood and latest celebrity relationship status, she was certainly applying it! She was oblivious at our shock at asking us to open our "textbooks" (really a compilation of gossip magazines) or at our irritation at calling us nincompoops for having allegedly poor "general knowledge". Almost as if the period bell sensed our discomfort, it rang warning us about the starting of our next class, indoor sports.

The first sentence to be uttered by Mr.Akushin was "Winning...therein lies your salvation. By hook or by crook it should be your only goal". Okay, so what happens to morals like honesty and integrity? He spent an hour explaining the cheats of chess and how to put magnets in carom coins to ensure winning. He actually even intricately dissected the parts of a dummy human body to show us the various parts which would be seriously injured in a game of tennis making the other player unable to play. It was a wondrous and joyous class except for the fact that the main objective of it was learning to cheat.

The only reason Mr.Akushin could detain us in his class for more than an hour was because Mr.Karnabhakum was as usual fast asleep. At least this kept him from boring us to death.

Mrs. Keikaiy was too busy applying lip gloss to even notice our arrival. When she finally bestowed upon us mere mortals the favour of looking directly at us we felt privileged (for those who are still wondering, of course we didn't feel privileged, on the contrary we felt worthless and insignificant). She raised her highly artificial eyebrows as if trying to recollect why she was being disturbed by a bunch of pesky kids. Finally remembering the reason she pointed towards the dressing rooms, separate for boys and girls. As we entered the unknown territory of the dressing rooms we finally saw it. It was like Disneyland for the fashionistas. Even a person like me who really does not care what they wear was in a daze. Cupboards full of clothes worthy of Milan fashion week weren't even the best part. The fountains of non-alcoholic champagne and tiers of strawberries while trying out the dresses was delicious and the icing on the cake. A few dresses were distributed to each girl by their personal attendants (yes personal attendants!) and dates written on them – to be worn according to the occasion. The dress assigned to me was a yellow one with threads made of pure gold attaching it to my arms and a diamond broach! How in the world did they know that yellow-out of all colours- suits me the best and that diamond is my lucky gem! The first lesson was ballroom dancing. They just had to go ahead and spoil it all! Dancing and me are the only example of two opposite forces that repel each other. My fond memories of dancing include stepping on my partner's foot and falling off the stage. Dancing to me is like willingly accepting a natural disaster. It was going to be a total catastrophe! Our partners were already decided. I had to dance with a boy named Ranvir Avasthi. The surname Avasthi rang a bell. Obviously! That's Ragini's last name. I stepped into the battlefield scared to find another enemy instead of a comrade.

The guy was tall, with blackish-brown hair and a complete carbon copy of Ragini. No doubt they were twins (yes the background check was already done). Now only if some more information could be found about these troublesome twins (sorry twin, yet). His tone, dialect and speech immediately gave away his relation to Ragini and that he was the 'male voice' talking to her the other day. He said, "Oh! So you are Pragya…" sensing my confusion he whispered, "…you aren't the only one capable of a successful background check … and a friendly advice, which might save your life in this school is not to be in Ragini's bad books. Oh boy! She is the one person who can rip apart her enemies". Thanks for the not-so-helpful tip I thought to myself and did not have a chance to voice my opinion as he had long disappeared. The guy reminded me of a rabbit in a magician's hat … he just went poof!

After the meeting with Ragini's sibling which bordered on normal and extraordinary I headed for the only class which could make maths and dancing look good… physical education…

I am not a warrior ninja princess, nor am I wonder woman. I do not, I repeat DO NOT like being taught sword fighting or mace throwing, nor do I like learning to jump 12 feet in the air. But did anyone pay any attention to my complaints, pleas and requests? No they did not. I felt as if I had attained salvation when the bell rang and we could finally get rid of the sports- crazy Mr.Dyuordhan. We made our way to our next class adorning our stinking sweaty clothes. Wonder what Mr.Avran would have to say about that…

Out of all teachers, Mr.Avran seemed the most prepared (with actual learning material). He even had all our clothes brought from our dorms so we could change from our sweaty clothes. I couldn't find anything eerie about him (yes! searching for weird habits in my teachers had become a trend for me in my new school). Wait, why was he wearing a hat when it was almost 90 degrees outside (not literally of course)? And not just an ordinary hat, a hhhuuuuggggeeeeee hat. It really was not my concern as long as he wasn't hiding an AK-47 or a rhinoceros under that hat. He had a slight Indian twang but was otherwise extremely expressive and proper while teaching my favourite subject. He gave us an assignment which was writing and enacting a play in a team. We were divided into two groups and while (thankfully!) Ragini wasn't in my team I got the second best thing a.k.a person, the mystery boy himself... Ranvir Avasthi. Hope I can recollect a few karate moves if he turns out to be a bigger jerk than his sister...

With that not-so-ordinary end I went to Mr.Sanak's class.

What's wrong with a bag which has the picture of a peacock on it? Apparently a lot. As soon as I entered Mr.Sanak immediately sent me back to my dorm to get a new bag. How rude! The rest of the class he went on and on and on and on...... about how science is the only force we should trust. Okay got the message, now you can get on with some real teaching, I felt like saying. But most probably those lines would have got me some vigorous hours in detention so I kept my lips sealed.

History is okay, maybe even good if I were to stretch the truth a little. A hot-headed...sorry a **volcano** headed teacher certainly did not help. She was in (what everyone had named them) one of her "moods". She was rumoured to have thrown a desk out of her window as some boy hadn't done his homework. The boy's name was Prahlad or something like that. I made a mental note to always complete her homework.

Have your teachers ever have a nasal tone and nails as sharp as claws or talons and to top it all, a weird eccentric hairdo? Apparently my geography teacher loved that idea. The most striking feature of Miss.Sukarphana's face was her nose. Not a real nose of course cause the real thing was lost under hundreds of layers of bandage. She looked like Pinocchio's evil twin sister. Had she never heard of cosmetic surgery? Unfortunately she caught me staring at her nose and made a beyond horrible sound with those talons screeching against the blackboard like claws digging into Satan's soul.

After all those classes –ranging from mildly eerie to disastrous-Dr.S surprised us with a treat to the library!!Okay, library might not sound the best but books certainly help calm down your mind and put a smile back on your face. After a nice and soothing read I was ready to face whatever new challenge this school threw at me. I screamed in my mind, "So what's next?" Big mistake, huge mistake.

Horrifying Homework

"Every deed done with hard work and persistence
reaps a reward...unless it is homework of course."

– Anonymous (wink wink)

I do not understand the deceptively relaxing phrases "calm
down and let life take its own path". Yeah right, the first
thing I should do when burdened by a bucketful of tests to
study for and a truckload of annoying homework is relax?!

After reaching the dorm we found huge stacks of papers.
Huge is a pathetic understatement, more like gigantic. It
had these weird assignments and was in two piles, one for
Nandini and one for me.

I was getting freaked out by just looking at this....stuff. It
wasn't out of ordinary really but just looking at homework
gives me the creeps.

So strange happenings, doesn't really stop worse things from
happening.

The Deceptively Dreary Day

"It never failed to amaze me how the most
ordinary day could be catapulted into the
extraordinary in the blink of an eye."

– Jodi Picoult, *Handle with Care*

Have you ever had one of those days? That day when you had everything-including the number of times you blink-planned. The day that was going to be perfect. Even your most hated foe couldn't spoil that day. I was having that kind of day.

Obviously, the universe couldn't help but mess up my day. The stars have become habituated at predicting a future where my day goes horribly wrong. So something (or some*one*) did ruin the day. Unfortunately, two someone rather than one did ruin my day. Who else? But the troublesome twins.

I was walking towards my dorm, minding my own business when I heard a scream coming in the opposite direction. I ran towards the voice. It sounded suspiciously like Nandini's…

<u>4hours later to what felt like the end of the world:</u>

Oh.My.God! I am going to kill Ragini once she comes out of the infirmary...and her own brother.

Let me begin at the beginning...it started with the burning of the books...

<u>4hours previous to the incident:</u>

When I reached all the screaming it wasn't Nandini who was screaming but Ragini was hysterically shouting. I smelt something burning. Then I saw the pile. That wretched girl was burning all my belongings in the middle of the auditorium. Then something stranger than all this happened Ranvir forcibly made her drink some liquid which made her convulse into fits and finally become unconscious. A book which wasn't burning hit Ranvir exactly on his head. I was marvelling at the throw until I realised it was me. We all froze. Maybe it was shock at seeing a person fall unconscious on the floor, maybe hitting the Avasthi siblings had become a habit. Who knows?

<u>Back to the present:</u>

Thankfully no one complained. Dr.S had continuously requested then tried to force me in the infirmary with Ragini. She thought I was "traumatised". But I didn't want to go. I couldn't face her after everything.

I smelt something burning. Then I saw the pile. That wretched girl was burning all my belongings in the middle of the auditorium.

Not The ... Tests!!

Do not rely completely on any other human
being, however dear. We meet all life's greatest
tests alone.

– Agnes Macphail

The one thing that makes homework look easy. The one
thing that makes grown men cry for their mommies. Well,
you guessed it! One point to you. It is ... tests. I am not
talking about class tests or even exams but the mere idea
of proving yourself against worthy competitors. Apparently
once this school starts, it doesn't rest. Because even with all
that was happening you have to give the ... test!

The test schedule was sent to us in our dormitory room. That horrible piece of paper read something like that:

TEST SCHEDULE FOR STANDARD IX AND X:

MONDAY (21ST AUGUST): **LITERATURE**

TUESDAY (22ND AUGUST): **LANGUAGE**

WEDNESDAY (23RD AUGUST): **MATHEMATICS**

THURSDAY (24TH AUGUST): **INDOOR SPORTS**

FRIDAY (25TH AUGUST): **PHYSICAL EDUCATION**

MONDAY (28TH AUGUST): **ETIQUETTES AND MANNERS**

TUESDAY (29TH AUGUST): **SCIENCE**

WEDNESDAY (30TH AUGUST): **GEOGRAPHY**

THURSDAY (31ST AUGUST): **HISTORY**

FRIDAY (1ST SEPTEMBER): **HINDI**

We had thirty days for ten examinations with an undecided portion, odd teachers, no preparation and a mysterious school. We were lost. Life was hopeless.

IDEA BANK - Draw, paint, doodle or write what you liked/disliked in this book. Leave notes for your friends or simply finish that maths sum you have been avoiding

The Lurking Loner

> "When you are a hero you are always running to
> save someone, sweating, worried and guilty.
> When you are a villain you are just lurking in the
> shadows waiting for the hero to pass by.
> Then you pop them in the head and go home...
> piece of cake."
>
> – James Marsters

I was on a cat-and-mouse chase for the last hour. The only problem was I hadn't the least idea whom I was chasing...

<u>An hour ago:</u>

I was humming a 'Titanic' song while climbing up the stairs to my dorm after the manners and etiquette class had just ended. Suddenly I saw a shadow and when I called out to him/her, the shadow disappeared. Finding that a little too out-of-ordinary I decided to investigate. While turning a corner I saw a piece of torn black silk. Why did that look so familiar? I heard footsteps shuffling behind me. Astonishingly when I turned around I saw nothing but a…a…black shoe. This was turning out to be Cinderella. I saw the mysterious shadow again. I did what any normal (a.k.a. overly curious) person would do in my position. I ran behind the figure.

Present time:

I would've continued my chase if I hadn't bumped into Dr.S. She was reading a book and I was running as fast as a non-athlete could and we collided. I was already in an embarrassing situation but to make matters worse she said, "Ranvir Avasthi, why are you trying to silently sneak away?" I should've guessed. His costume for the day in the etiquettes and manners class was a BLACK SILK COAT.

PS: I told you that we had to wear a shapeless sack.

Rendevous with the Rival

"I embrace my rival, but only to strangle him.

– Jean Racine"

The Avasthi twins never fail to surprise me. While one burn my books, the other lurks around in shadows trying to hide... but from whom? He certainly looked scared, stripped of his air of confidence and poise by Dr.S. He looked like he had committed a heinous crime. I prayed that whatever he had done had nothing to do with me this time. Due to some extraordinary reasons I felt personally threatened and targeted by those troublesome twins from the moment I met them. He had started perspiring with terror. Why was he so terrified? Let me rephrase my question... What made him so scared? I know that Ragini was still being treated by the school nurse with the assistance of Dr.S (who after having several Ph. Ds also was a medical practitioner). The now pale boy was stuttering something illegible until we finally decided to follow him. He rushed towards the infirmary. Ragini was the only one in there and she was having some sort of fits. She was pointing accusingly in my direction. Finally Ranvir literally pushed me out of the room screaming that I was "affecting" Ragini, whatever that means. Granted that they were one of the earliest students in the school and belonged to the senior-most batch, they had no right to throw temper-tantrums because of no apparent reason. All of a sudden, an announcement rang throughout the school by Dr.S. It said, "All teachers report to my office, its time".

The Stunning Secret

"All journeys have secret destinations of which
the traveler is unaware".

– Martin Buber

"Still round the corner there may wait,
a new road or a secret gate."

– J. R. R. Tolkien

"The human heart has hidden treasures,
in secret kept, in silence sealed; the thoughts,
the hopes, the dreams, the pleasures,
whose charms were broken if revealed".

– Charlotte Bronte

We were told to assemble in the auditorium. "What next?"
Was the question in all our minds. For once all two thousand
brains in the hall were thinking together. All of a sudden the
lights dimmed and a huge projector materialised out of thin

air. Chairs appeared beneath us and the speaker boomed. The chairs really did help as we stumbled due to shock after hearing the song which played on the microphone. The phrase "IT'S A SECRET!" and the song went something like this,

"Being evil is good,
Being evil is great,
It doesn't want to make you wait,
Being naughty is best,
It makes you stand out from the rest,
It gives you a unique personality,
Evil needs no nationality.
Being evil is good,
Being evil is great,
It makes you want to embrace life,
It makes idiots wanna brace thine.
There is an evil in everyone you just need to find it."

As if that wasn't enough another-radically opposite song-sung by the honey – sweet voice of Dr.S,

"Being good is good,
Being good is great,
It doesn't want to make you wait,
Being nice is the best,
It makes you stand out from the rest,
It gives you a unique personality,
Good needs no nationality.
Being good is good,
Being good is great,
It makes you wanna embrace life,

It makes wrong-doers wanna brace thine.
There is good in everyone you just need to find it."

Everyone froze. If pin-drop silence existed I could feel it. Finally with a dazzling white flame setting the stage on fire (no pun intended) the time-wrap ended. Next came a golden chariot. Then there was an old queenly dressing table with an arrow on it, a mace, an old shawl, a huge bed, a grand throne, a pile of old scriptures, a humongous dice and a blood stained knife on a beautiful wrap-around dress. What was happeni…?

I did not even get to finish my question as the students had just noticed something extremely interesting (Ah… finally the use of that word after using ostentatious, vile and disgusting). Ragini was screaming something at the top of her voice while running towards us. It sounded like "Cylcl… Cy….cl..n…Cyclone!"

No one believed her until we saw it with our very own eyes. What? Were we in school or in hell? (What's the difference?) There was a mini-stampede with everyone trying to run away from the huge black cloud which looked like cyclone (but one can never be too certain!). All of a sudden we froze. Not willingly, but because our feet became chained on its own.

Finally the teachers arrived on stage. We stared at them with a confused expression. We couldn't see their faces or attires due to the dim lighting. A spotlight shined on Dr.S' face blinding all of us. Wait…that was not a spotlight, that was a halo… like the one angels have. She was wearing a white saree…and was that a…a…crown? Her pet swan looked quite content on her lap. Finally all of the teachers were visible due to the unknown light. But what exactly were they wearing? Everyone except Miss.Rathmana (who was dressed in that old shawl) was dressed in princely clothes with the men and women both wearing an obnoxious amount of jewellery and both not following the school dress code by being either too gorgeously or too austerely dressed.

Dr.S, interrupting my imaginations said, "Children, as students it is your duty to help your school, and as a human, to help the world. Both need you". She paused, "I know, it is disappointing to know that someone lied to you but sometimes it is for your own good…I am requesting you to help out this school by telling you about its truth." I knew there was something wrong with this school, I thought to myself. Dr.S continued, "…you all are well aware of Indian mythology, the one with Gods and Goddesses defeating the "seemingly evil". After reading a mythological book or watching such a film have you ever reflected on the villain's situation or ever have a hunch that it's not just another story based on the writer's imagination but a non-fictional fact. Well, one thing is for sure…that stories of, about and in India tend to be true. So, why not these stories? Science is factual, but there are people who made science … such extraordinary people were called 'Gods' and now enjoy a heavenly abode. Before writing me off as another crazy professor, you should know –how I came to know all this 'stuff'. It is because I am… one of them. I am Saraswati." She paused to let that not-at-all-surprising (read as-life extractingly shocking) news sink in. "But tonight is not about the good guys but the bad ones." She continued "Everyone deserves a second chance, so I decided to neglect the ideas of my friends and family of the gruesome techniques of permanently killing the villains defeated by them. I decided to give them an equally painful but more rewarding and constructive work…… raising and schooling a bunch of reckless teenagers. Over the years we were sure that no other danger was going to rise up against humanity… but it did. We need you…you…you and every student, who is also the future of this country and the world, to rise up and fight. Fight for your family, friends, acquaintances and even strangers. Never feel too afraid to change or stand up for yourself…and to demonstrate this I would like each of the teachers to express a more humane side of them-which isn't usually included in the stories. So I would like to start with Mr.Avran, Oh! My mistake…Mr. Ravan…

... I would like it if you all would repeat
after me the oath of secrecy.

The Ostentatious Oath

It is not the oath that makes us believe the man,
but the man the oath.

– Aeschylus

Unfortunately, in today's world we have to be reminded
that the power of an oath derives from the fact that
in it we ask God to bear witness to the promises we
make with the implicit expectation that He will hold us
accountable for the manner in which we honour them.

– James L. Buckley

"Before I begin my speech I would like it if you all
would repeat after me the oath of secrecy." The manner
in which Mr.Avran...I mean Mr.Ravan said *like* it was
understandable he wanted to say **have to.** Then the oath
taking ceremony started.

"WE, THE STUDENTS OF THIS SCHOOL WOULD
  SOLEMNLY PROMISE ON OUR
WORSE SECRET
FAVOURITE STUFFED TOY
MOST AMAZING BOOK
ENTERING TEENAGE
THINGS THAT SCARED US WHEN WE WERE
  KIDS (AND STILL DO!) A.K.A WORST FEAR
THE AWESOME VACATIONING SPOT
HATRED OF HOMEWORK
THAT WE SHALL NEVER EVER EVER EVER
  EVER EVER EVER EVER EVER EVER EVER
  EVER DISCLOSE THE SECRET IDENTITY OF
  THIS SCHOOL OR ITS TEACHERS TO ANY
  OUTSIDER.
IF WE BREAK THIS BOND ALL FORCES OF HELL
  SHALL BE UNLEASHED ON US AND WE
  WOULD NOT BE ABLE TO DO ANYTHING
  ABOUT IT."

After this beyond odd oath, started the true introductions of the teachers. First up was Avran- oh! I mean Ravan...

"Now those of you have read the Ramayana you know me...somewhat. For those who don't, I was the king of Lanka, killed some people, and kidnapped others blah blah blah. In reality my worst decision was over-pampering my little sister. Sorry Surpanakha. But as an elder brother I just performed my duty towards her. Just for the record, that Sita was kidnapped and allegedly tortured was staying with my queen Mandodari and I treated her like my daughter. Her husband was too overzealous about war but I had planned to leave her a long time before the so called "great war". Really the war was routine procedure then… I have no clue why people make such a great fuss about it now. Ram and I are actually on cordial terms now. Hanuman seems a little cross but he is a good monke…I mean boy. Those days were all about war … I too would have become a doctor, teacher or lawyer. Argument without bloodshed wasn't a possibility in those days. Um…I don't know what else to say but just want to conclude with the fact that before judging, if someone walks a mile in their shoes only then you earn the right to be judgemental."

Next person on stage was Ms.Sukarphana (Surpanakha)… the fun fact about her was that she was also known as one of the reasons for one of the greatest Indian wars…oh you thought 1857? I meant the Ramayana…

She started in her rather nasally voice, "I have been accused, snapped at … and in extreme scenarios even slashed at with a sword. It's really weird that people expected women to be perfect in a day and an age with neither liposuction nor salons. Obviously, black magic was my only option to look charming and pretty and attractive. I am sure no girl in this room would blame me for trying to look like Katrina in front of two handsome guys building a hut. I can't really say I was blameless but trust me life as a modern day working woman is heaven as compared to an olden day princess. I wish I was so lucky as to be born in the 21st century and choose what I would like to do…not what I was supposed to do." Dr.S quickly added- "Oh! And we would like to thank Duryodhana for lending us one of his grand palaces".

Call me ADHD* but I was feeling restless and I really wanted to throw something at the stage...I was shocked, to say the least. My courage, pride, level headed nature everything betrayed me at the sight of fictional characters** popping out from a story written thousands of years ago. I edged towards the door to escape this madness. Dr.S was bemused to see me leave and looked at me-directly in the eye. I felt a chill run up my spine, my body froze, my fingers gripped the seat, my head started spinning and I felt numb as darkness overcame me...

*=Attention deficit hyperactive disorder

**=How can anyone be sure?

The Stupendous Stupa

You can't build a great building on a weak
foundation. You must have a solid foundation if
you're going to have a strong superstructure.

– Gordon B. Hinckley

Twice…the number of times I had fainted in this school. I think I might be having a…condition. But the second time felt different. When Dr.S looked at me it felt as if someone had laid bare in front of them my soul, mind and dissected my entire existence in those few, negligible seconds. It was as if we connected on a whole new level and my thoughts merged with hers. Then the weirdest thing happened… Dr.S (or Sarawati…as you like it) vanished and in her place stood….me. It was like looking into a mirror except there was none. Then "The return of the fainting girl…" took place. I woke up in the infirmary and was greeted with the not-so comforting and eerie sight of all the teachers staring down at me.

They all looked at me like I was a frog in a biology class…
sad about my fate but curious nonetheless.

Trust me … staring into a couple of stern, confused faces of
weird adults is not my idea of "recovery".

Nevertheless it was the situation and I had to deal with it.
All of a sudden I was lifted into the air by a magical force
which twisted my poor little body in angles a yoga teacher
would fear to attempt. My feet were thrust up in the air with
my head dangling below and my exposed tongue turning
rougher by unwillingly tasting the dry hospital air. All the
teachers were inspecting me like a pig for slaughter. Dr.S was
sitting quietly in a far corner with a blank expression on her
face. Finally I asked *"WHAT IS GOING ON?"* …I mean
I shouted, to which they all looked at me with an amused
expression and nodded their heads in uncanny succession
as if approving the question.

Then Sukarphana…oh shoot…Miss Surpanakha, exclaimed
in surprise, she said… *"sA … gauravavat … preSaNa?sA
Azrita ekam?!"*

"से…गौरववत्… प्रेषण? से आश्रित एकम्?!"

Repeated most others.

Why is she speaking in Sankskrit…why do I know she is
speaking in Sanskrit…being unaware of the language and
its nuances, I could complete her half-broken exclamations

of shock. She said, *"SHE is important for the mission? SHE is the one who is supposed to save the world?!"*

It was kind of harsh how little belief my teacher had on me but being utterly confused already I had nothing to say.

Then Dr.S walked up to me and introduced me to all the other teachers whose introduction I had slept through... literarily.

It went something like this.... "So this is Mr.Akushin a.k.a Shakuni, greatest chess player, evil mastermind behind the Mahabharat...actually a loyal brother, uncle and patriot (of his country Gandhara). Then Mr.Sanak or Kansa, Krishna's uncle, imprisoned his sister and her husband, killed most of their children...actually another over-confident person ready to change their fate. Miss Rathmana or Manthara, evil conspirator, poisoned queen Kaikeyi (who we will come to in a second) that her son was the only one fit to be king... actually a serial gossip girl, faithful to her mistress, slightly greedy of position elevation. Mrs. Kaikeyi a supposedly sly and power hungry wife, betrayed her extended family, caused misery to the kingdom, root cause of her husband's untimely death but what is lesser known about Kaikeyi is that well ... she is Kaikeyi...easily influenced, living in a self-created bubble, brave (as she once saved her husband on the battlefield). Duryodhana was subjected to one of the epitomes of unfairness. He was the eldest son of the eldest brother and deserved the crown but due to his foolish, hasty and egoistic decisions lost his birth right. Hence it is said that a person's choices in life matter more than anything else. Then comes Shakad or Daksha the pioneer of over concerned dads, with a twisted and evil climax with his daughter (who was married to a God!) dying. My feisty teacher Kaholi introduced herself as Holika, a fire demoness (oh, that explains the fiery attitude) who tried to kill her nephew... well in her defence that guy wasn't best crown prince. Mr.Karnabhakum just resembled the legends of Kumbhakarna that he didn't even have to introduce himself (what with the uncannily similar name and sloth like sleeping habits!)

Realisation dawned upon me...all their pseudonyms were anagrams of their real names...like Karnabhakum for Kumbhakarna and Rathmana for Manthara etc. Talk about originality.

As usual, before anyone explained anything to me I was ushered into the auditorium ... and yes I was still wearing my hospital gown...

It's scary to stand in a rag. I know...I know...we students stand in rags everyday during assembly *ahem* sorry uniforms. But standing in a rag-like hospital gown, on a stage, in front of hundreds of confused students is especially terrifying.

Considering the mammoth amount of weirdness in the school...I wasn't really surprised to see a massive rock in the middle of the room.

This school throws surprises at me faster than I eat pizza (a.k.a the speed of light). So a huge stupa in the room was alright ... until it started glowing. A humming noise was produced from the rock. In the chaos I stealthily climbed off the stage and walked towards the middle of the room.

As if in a trance Nandini walked towards the stage…she was wrapped in a blue curtain of light and lifted about ten feet in the air. A picture of Surpanakha appeared next to her. All of a sudden she dropped to the ground with a thud as the stupa lost its glow… as if someone had pulled the plug in a tube light. Dr.S literally jumped onto the stage and announced, "Sorry children! I apologise that you had to face the stupa unprepared! This stupa is going to analyse your potential, characteristics and mentality and enhance your qualities, assigning you a mentor with similar traits and outlook who can properly guide you. So welcome to stand trial before this stupendous stupa!"

It started to glow again…this time a golden-orange hue of fire and enclosed Ragini in its fiery bright cocoon and displayed a photograph of Holika next to her. The process repeated itself for Ranvir who glowed within a deep red light, and his side had the visage of Ravan next to him. At the end of all the selections I felt an instant attraction towards…the rock. I was pulled towards it by an imaginary force and was lifted in the air. Inside a white sheet of bright light I saw Dr.S…I mean Sarawati next to me…and I am sure I heard the stone *sigh*. I felt energy surge into me and my pathetic clothing vanish. Rich fabric and soothing sensations rejuvenated my weary body and something like a tiara was placed on my now tangle free smooth, silky and flowing hair.

I was lost in the imaginary world where everything seemed possible and I seemed powerful until I was jerked back into reality by a ten feet drop. I landed in an unseemly fashion i.e., on a cloud instead of smack on my face. After all, the cloud was the least of my worries. Simultaneously all the students' clothes changed into royal, rich and classily beautiful clothing. Yet I noticed none of them wore a crown/tiara like me. I read the school motto on the ceiling of the auditorium realising … for the first time…that it was always written in Sanskrit. I felt memories gushing into my brain. The first man…discovery of reading and writing…civilization…a princess learning to play a veena…Lord Pareshurama wielding an axe…Lord Ram lifting a bow…Draupadi's birth …The First War of Independence-1857… … J.K. Rowling, sitting in an apron and writing on a tissue paper... Laxmi Devi complaining about unfair usage of WIFI on my part? ...and yesterday's News hour? Basically vague bits and pieces of Dr.S' memories…throughout time. Experiences in this school sure can get mind-bogglingly crazy…

IDEA BANK - Draw, paint, doodle or write what you liked/disliked in this book. Leave notes for your friends or simply finish that maths sum you have been avoiding

Predatory Pets

"What is a pet?"
"An animal that we do not eat."
"We call those children."

– The Croods

List of things Pragya Mukherjee did not expect:

1. Everything that happens in this school.
2. (RE-READ THE ABOVE LINE).
3. (I HATE REPEATING MYSELF).

Teachers give out free stationery for projects … our "educators" gave out…pets.

You know how everyone seemed to have a pet/companion/over-protective friend/guardian angel in ancient India? Well it was no coincidence.

I was shivering with anticipation when my turn came around. I DID NOT want a TIGER like Ranvir, nor a dove like Nandini. I DEFINITELY DID NOT want a rat as Ragini did, serves her right)...

Fingers crossed, head spinning, you would think I am giving an exam.

Phew, yes, yay, wow, fantastic … no I haven't lost my mind…it is just that I got the cutest pet EVER. My parrot winked back at me when I cuddled him with relief. The green colour blended with his red and yellow feathers giving him a royal appearance. Thank God I did not get a swan (they bite, ouch!).

Apparently being heart-wrenchingly cute does not stop him from being vicious…

...it is just that I got the cutest pet EVER. My parrot winked back at me when I cuddled him with relief.

IDEA BANK - Draw, paint, doodle or write what you liked/disliked in this book. Leave notes for your friends or simply finish that maths sum you have been avoiding

Bull's eye!

Preposterous Preparations

The best preparation for tomorrow is doing your
best today.

– H. Jackson Brown, Jr.

I officially agree normal schoolwork is, was and will be better. This is the worst. All that training continuously reminds me why I never chose physical education as a subject. Who asks a fourteen year old to lift a sword heavier than her weight after a Sunday brunch…who does that?!The only weapon I could tolerate was the bow and arrow which had slipped into the curve of my hand just before my thumb and adjusted perfectly. I could feel its oak-wood humming against my sweaty palm and, as if, magically directing my hand to the target. I could feel the slender arrow slip through its firm hold and hit the bull's eye in one shot. The effect was ethereal…I had never felt more pride…I could shoot (NOT JUST PHOTOS!!!).

Dr.S congratulated me and left the room. Almost everyone had gone-off to lunch by now and that could explain why I screamed like a cheerleader with a broken toenail when a husky voice said, "Congrats!" I should have known … happiness is short-lived when you are on the same campus as Ranvir Avasthi. He slipped on my bow (without asking me might I add!) and shot an arrow with the ease that the Kardashians shoot selfies. I hate him with the totality of the hatred that courses through these veins. But yet there is something about that guy…

My thoughts were interrupted when Ragini threw a mace (YES, A MACE!) at my face, which missed barely by inches. I was touched by how humbly she had given up her "official post" as centre-of-attraction (NOT!!). "Oops! Sorry ", she smiled a million dollar smile, made of counterfeit notes, of course. "Did I interrupt something?", she said glaring at her brother who seemed to notice the shiny black marble floor for the first time. I ughed and left the room.

I love reading. I truly do. I live for it … but anything but STUDY BOOKS. Which idiot had the brilliant idea of printing 21 fat volumes of "Battle Strategy" and 12 of "How to win a war – For dummies"??

"I HAVE TO FIGHT IN A SARI?!" I had screamed this line every 5 minutes ensuring that every living soul on the island heard me. "Yes", said Dr.S for the 947621… (I have stopped counting…) th time. She held the mauve angavastram for me, "प्रेक्षणीयतम!*" Exclaimed that same husky voice who stood with a gaping mouth as I entered a hall full of students, wearing a sari. I blushed. Dr.S smiled and told me that I remind her of her old friend रती**

(*=most beautiful)

(**=goddess of love)

<u>An hour later:</u>

We were preparing for a war that we knew NOTHING AT ALL about. So yeah, it was kind of like the mathematics exam.

This time Mr.Akushin alias Shakuni (of all the people) started off, but not before adjusting his new clothes many times and spoke in an amazingly rich and royal voice: "Now all of you ... children. (He wanted to say brats, I just know it). I know that your tiny little brains (he was just so tired of flattery and smooth talking) cannot comprehend what is going on but try to keep up. A ... monster called विषाक्तमनस्साक्षिन् is trying to invade our nation and our lives. Before you all kill yourselves with curiosity about the name it means it means 'poisoned conscience'. I know it sounds obvious and simple but evil could exist right under your noses and you wouldn't bat an eyelid..." there was something creepy about the way he winked after that "... This "monster"..." woohoo air quotes, "... is made up of all the evil extracted from simple minds like mine." *Ahem* says Ravan (trying very hard not to laugh at how Mr.Shakuni thinks he has a SIMPLE mind). Ravan then starts speaking by saying "This evil was churned with poison from the largest and most venomous snake. It is difficult to destroy as even the GODS can only contain it...not so great now, are they? Well they leave it up to us to find a ...*solution* for their problem." The way he said Gods, he could have been given the national award for sassiest tone. He smirked as he finished causing Dr.S to hurriedly say, "Thank you sir for that ...enlightening speech."

I am calling the monster Vissy. It's so much easier.

I was thrust unto the stage while Dr.S (or Devi Saraswati as I should really start calling her) asked me to start the victory chant (which somehow I knew, do not ask questions):

कथमपि मया विजयः प्राप्तव्यम्

(Somehow I must attain victory)

मृत्यु हि उपपत्ति

(Death for (a) cause)

अभिगोप्तृ अस्माकम् पृथ्वीशता

(Protecting our kingdom)

विनाशिन् अस्माकम् शत्रु

(Destroying our foes)

स्नेह अस्माकम्

क्षोणी

(Love our people)

युद्ध यावत्पर्यन्तम् मर्यादा

(Fight till (the) end)

Pretty inspirational!

Having a quiet moment at Metamorphosis was impossible as I was pulled…no jerked backwards and pulled back backstage. Dr.S looked stunned, confused and basically betrayed her usual demeanour. She looked scatterbrained at times, dignified at most but seldom stunned. She started the first not-so carefully prepared speech in a long time, "Now I know…they weren't misled…you ARE the one…it has sensed you *it is coming.*" Genuinely tired of confused instructions and puzzled exclamations asked…no commanded her to begin at the beginning…

You know those stories that are really really short and sweet. Well this one just wasn't like those.

The story (OR WHAT I ~~HEARD~~ UNDERSTOOD OF IT):

LONG LONG LONG LONG LONG LONG LONG LONG LONG LONG *gasp* THERE WERE WARS, FIGHTS AND ECCENTRIC BARGAINS. NOW ALL THESE CREATED TWO TYPES OF PEOPLE-WINNERS AND THE PEOPLE WHO STAND AT THE CORNER OF THE TIME -OUT ZONE, AND CRY, CALLED LOSERS. THE WINNERS WANTED THE "TIME-OUT ZONE"(CALLED HELL BY DEAR FRIENDS)TO FILL BEFORE COLLECTIVELY PUNISHING THE HYPERACTIVE LOSERS.

FAST FORWARD TO A FEW MILLENIA:… THERE AT MIDNIGHT SAT A COUNCIL. NO THIS ISN'T A HISTORY LESSSON (WELL IT KINDA IS). THIS COUNCIL WAS A GROUP OF SPECIALLY CELEBRATED & APPOINTED MINISTERS, AKA, SCAM *giggling noises*. THE SCAMS (THE WINNERS OF EARTH-SHATTERING WARS AND CELESTIAL HUMANS) WERE APPOINTED TO PUT TO JUSTICE "THE - CITIZENS (creating) UNFORGIVABLE TURMOIL (on) EARTH" i.e., C.U.T.E*more giggling noises*. "NOW NOTHING PORTRAYS ETERNAL DAMNATION LIKE MODERN MISERABLE TEENS? "THEY THOUGHT." LETS OPEN A SCHOOL", THEY SAID. BUT THE EARTH WAS STILL PROGRESSING. "I HAVE YET TO CREATE WIFI",

SAID THE CREATOR. "I HAVE TO PROTECT THE HUMAN RACE EVERY DAY FROM ITSELF TO HELP IT SURVIVE ..." COMMENTED THE PRESERVER/PROTECTOR, "...THESE STUDENT SUICIDES ARE GOING TO DRIVE ME CRAZY!!" THE DESTROYER SCOFFED, "YOU WHINY KIDS THINK YOU HAVE PROBLEMS? I HAVEN'T SLEPT PEACEFULLY, DUE TO THOSE TERRORISTS, MINDLESS VIDEO GAMES, CONSCIENCE-LESS PEOPLE AND ADULTERATED MILK, I AM EITHER OVERWORKED OR UNDERWORKED BECAUSE I HAVE FORGOTTEN WHAT TO DESTROY."

BUT WHAT USE WILL IT BE? THEY COULDN'T SPEND 50 LAKH CRORE GOLD COINS ON A USELESS SCHOOL ARGUED KUBER.

NARAD MUNI, AN UNLIKELY PARTICIPANT RAISED HIS HAND AND STARTED JUMPING. "LET'S KEEP AN EXCEPTIONALLY TALENTED QUOTA...DIFFERENT SKILLS FOR EVERYONE! AND BRAINWASH THEIR DISGUSTINGLY INNOCENT MIND TO FIGHT THE UPRISING EVIL FOR US... A WIN-WIN SITUATION!" SHOUTS OF NARAYAN FILLED THE CELESTIAL HALL. SARASWATI DEVI WITH HER UNBREAKABLE LOGIC INTERJECTED, "ISN'T IT A LITTLE UNFAIR AND HYPOCRITICAL FOR THE C.U.T.E.(s) TO TEACH THE CHILDREN? WHO WILL LEAD? WHAT WILL THEY TEACH?" HER MOTHER SPOKE UP, "YOU MY DEAR WILL SEE TO THAT...YOU WERE

ALWAYS SO …KNOWLEDGEABLE, EVEN AS A CHILD…THE ONE WITH YOUR ESSENCE WILL LEAD." HER SISTER SPOKE UP, "MOM NO WHY DOES DIDI HAS TO GO?" "BECAUSE I SAID SO, TRUST ME, MUMMY DEAREST IS HERE, DON'T YOU LITTLE GODDESS' FEAR."

"CAN WE CHANGE THE NURSERY RHYME STATION?" THOUGHT ALL THE GODS.

SARASWATI HAD MADE UP HER MIND. THEY SAY KNOWLEDGE ACCEPTS NEW CONCEPTS BUT SARASWATI HAD INDIRECTLY GIVEN HER WORD. GENERATIONS CAME AND WENT, PEOPLE WERE BORN EVERY DAY BUT NO ONE HAD EVER HONOURED A PROMISE LIKE SARASWATI DID. SHE AGREED TO THE UNIMAGINABLE…TO BE A GODDESS AMONG MORTALS. THATS WHERE THE SAYING –KNOWLEDGE LIVES WITHIN US, COMES FROM.

A DOCTOR OF PHILOSOPHY IN – WELL EVERYTHING…DR.S WAS HER PSEUDONYM.

SHE DESCENDED AMIDST POLLUTION AND CORRUPTION WITH THE SAME GRACE THAT A LOTUS BLOOMS IN MUCK…SHE WANTED TO MAKE A PERFECT WORLD WITH A SWISH OF HER HAND…UNTIL SHE DISCOVERED 90 PERCENT OF HER POWERS HAD BEEN REVOKED. THIS WAS GOING TO BE TOUGH.

Now that we were back to the future I saw her for the brave warrior that she was…giving up her heavenly lifestyle, actually.

Back to the future: Whoa….That was one creepy story.

Funny thing about creepy stories…they are always cliff-hangers, mysterious and shady but this one ended with me holding a brown, filthy stone…yak!

You rub a lamp, but what do you do with a pathetic non-wish granting stone? I thought after a touching and inspiring story I would get something more than a stone….but no…

Apparently it was impossible for ANYTHING to happen in this school without it completely freaking me out. So of course the stupid stone had to burn my hand and start glowing. I dropped it and immersed my hand in a nearby bucket filled with water while Dr.S watched with a quizzical brow. I felt my stomach churning and was certain I was going to throw up until I removed my hand to find the skin join each other forming a fresh layer covering up the burnt surface.

So was I like immortal? "Umm…just invincible", Dr.S' voice called out. Of course! She could now read my thoughts. I loved being Supermanwoman. Then I noticed the teeny, tiny problem. I had wings. There is no subtle way to put this…I looked like a hatchling with purple wings. My "human form" was intact, but I looked kind of scary and weird … especially when the wings dropped off within sometime to be replaced by a white coloured pair.

List of normal thing that had happened today (note the sarcasm):

- Creepy ancient story
- Semi-immortality
- Purple coloured wings
- White coloured wings
- Making a list of all the crazy things that have happened today.
- Re-read above point!

…I looked like a hatchling with purple wings.
My "human form" was intact,
but I looked kind of scary and weird …

IDEA BANK - Draw, paint, doodle or write what you liked/disliked in this book. Leave notes for your friends or simply finish that maths sum you have been avoiding

The Battle

I don't really like battles,
but sometimes it is the only way

– Metamorphosis

I don't really like battles, but sometimes it is the only way. A huge gigantic snake emerged from the ground and spat fire at the onlookers and killed everyone. Unfortunately, in real life – battles are hard. Like harder then maths homework or exercise on a river filled with piranhas. They are exhausting and not really guilt-free. Battles are like English class being cancelled to accommodate an extra maths class OH THE HORROR! I hate anything that harms another human but when the fight is against something that I know nothing about…I just don't know. While I was thinking all of this, my wrist clenched something in front of my face and as if by reflex I caught it. It was a dart…a poisoned dart. The battle had begun.

You would think that being in a battle would be like super stressful … but it wasn't IT WAS CRAZILY, SCARILY

STRESSFUL. Unfortunately Vissy was nowhere to be seen and nor was his so called army. Suddenly I felt a prick on my back, then another, a third all before I turned around. My last words before fainting were, "Ranvir..."

I know what you all are thinking, "She faints a lot!" Let us review the situation...a poisonous dart flew to my face, my semi-friend threw it (as was obvious by me fainting... keep up folks!), I am in a dark room covered in a liquid which smells suspiciously like petroleum. So to sum it up I am experiencing the same kind of trauma I do during my exams. "No pressure". A candle lighted close to my face, Ranvir Avasthi's fake – face appeared before it... and here I thought his sister was the evil one. I stared at him with a murderous look (or whatever courage I could muster...hey, give the kid a break). He finally spoke, "Aww, I pity you trusting everyone so easily. You thought Ragini would harm you because she is hot-tempered? She is just a kid, and a jealous one. You, a lesser being from a lesser world are no match for my master, Vissy...uh...I mean... विषाक्तमनस्साक्षिन् sir. He will mash – up your mind and churn your essence..." While Ranvir continued with this puke-worthy recipe for my mind I finally understood what had happened...poisoned conscience...it all made sense... Vissy had poisoned Ranvir's conscience and made it part of his essence. All of a sudden a memory resurfaced ...a song my grandmother used to sing to me at bedtime...I started humming the tune, I didn't remember the full thing so I sang out phrases I basically rapped for my life, this was a true rap battle (pun intended). I started singing rapidly.

... Ranvir Avasthi's fake – face appeared before it...
and here I thought his sister was the evil one.

The song told you to get rid of evil and to embrace life and an additional phrase told you not to kill your friend (helpfully added by me!). My vocal chords had turned to shreds when Ranvir's pupils dilated and he seemed to be getting back to normal. Good point: He would not try to kill me. Bad point: The candle in his hand fell on my petroleum doused self. My long top caught fire and I was thinking that I better get a VIP fast pass to heaven. The now goofy, not- so-composed and VERY panicky Ranvir tried to stop the flames which caused him some third degree burns. Surprisingly I seemed unharmed, not that I am complaining. I then remembered Dr.S' words, "Um…just invincible". Yeah Vissy, the game is on. When we reached the campus (yes under Vissy's spell Ranvir had chosen a location 10 km away). I couldn't even shout at him seeing as how once the spell was over he needed glasses to see and hence walk. It was worse than babysitting a four year old. I had to answer his million apologies to make him feel better while handling my burning top (Yep, extra flammable, WHO DOES THAT?!). Everyone was surprised to see a girl covered in soot and a boy rapidly blowing at his hand to cool them. His sister angrily snatched him from my side and poured water on his burns. Now I know why she is always so angry.

... I knew that the brother-sister duo
looked out for one another...

I was scared. Vissy (I have got to stop calling ~~him~~ it that) had already planted a mole/agent INSIDE the academy. He is vicious rather vissy-ous (bad pun…I know). Vissy is so snaky…considering that he is a snake it shouldn't have been surprising when Ranvir was reciting some odd incidents and encounters when he was under the snake's influence. So basically he was like a snake charmer in reverse. But keeping these weird concepts aside I listened intently to what seemed like a new Ranvir. Thankfully he got his spectacles back and Ragini had softened (very, very little) and was helping treat his burns. I was like, that is sooooo sweeett but considering it is Ragini I dare not mention this but now I knew that the brother-sister duo looked out for one another and Ragini must have noticed something was wrong with her brother and hence the extra sour attitude. Now that everything was normal (almost) she actually smiled (almost).

"Such sentiment! Such emotion! How sweet! It was as if you all do not have impending disaster and doomsday to look forward too." Hey, my conscience was not so loud. Then I realised that it wasn't my conscience but a voice on the public address system. It was inside the school.

All the people listened to the voice as if in a trance. Shockingly, I was unaffected by the disgusting slithery, sugar-coated voice……a snake who speaks English. That is a first. All of a sudden a disco ball appeared and started spreading multicoloured light across the floor, a chunk of the first floor descended gracefully while a peppy Bollywood song played in the background. Or maybe a pug faced snake fell from the first floor whose floor had dissolved due to its corrosive venom. Most probably the second as I was dizzy and possibly hallucinating. Then the doggie like snake (YES IT LOOKED LIKE A BULLDOG AND NO IT WAS NOT CUTE AS IT WAS DARK BROWN AND BOTTLE GREEN WITH FANGS!) said, "Hello, old friend", before spewing venom at me.

Jokes on you, I am invincible I thought. Jokes on me, the venom still stung like the attack of a thousand bees.

I remembered my bow and arrow, prayed a little for it to at least hurt the snake like a needle. I aimed. The sassy snake, "Really, this is the best you can do?" "No, this is!" Said Ragini before hitting him with a mace in between his eyes. Ouch! That certainly shook him. I then noticed that none of the teachers were there in the battlefield. I thought it was one of those moments when the teachers were going to be like, "Life is a battle that you have to fight on your own". Thankfully Dr.S proved me wrong by landing on a giant swan. Giant like two or three shopping centres had been stuffed inside him. "Dessert …" said Vissy, "…how thoughtful". I was starting to hate the snake.

I threw down my bow and arrow and went to face the snake: woman to creature.

Adrenalin rushes are great. They make you do things you normally would run away from like a jet. What was I thinking charging at a snake like that? Dr.S helped me by throwing a spear at me (which thankfully didn't impale me!). I caught the spear like a warrior, jumped like a ninja and fell on the snake's head rather awkwardly like…well me. Vissy seemed pissed. I threw my entire weight at him while jumping on his slimy skull. The only problem…he had no skull. I slipped through his thin layer of slimy pinkish green skin and got a view of his brain while sliding into his stomach (which was surprisingly quite big) and slipped right into his stomach. My only thought at that moment was-funny, how he wanted to eat me up and I ended up in his stomach.

Disclaimer: Do not try to find a giant snake like thing and end up in its stomach without expert supervision (or with).

I was stuck in that awful, slimy, stinky place long enough to have a neighbourhood barbeque until I finally came out of its stomach with its GROSS ALERT vomit. Apparently swallowing me had drained him of its strength and it had fallen on the floor before getting rid of me from itself and vaporising off.

I thought that is it. I was like, this should end now. This has ended we are safe.

BOOM BOOM……..that my friend is the sound of us being not at all safe, rather very unsafe as our school started shaking and a pillar almost was crushing Nandini. I pushed her aside and my hand was stuck under the pillar. A transparent layer of magic and my slowly faltering willpower were the only thing that kept me from being nicknamed one armed Joe. Ranvir and his mentor Mr.Ravan finally came to my aid and pushed the pillar off me. I asked them, "How?!". Ranvir just said, "Glad I was paying attention to the school guide…remember the wishing well? Well-pun intended-it works after all". Some childish part of me wanted to try it out but the relatively sane part told me to focus on the battle. Wiser words of counsel had never been said (by me to myself) as just then I heard that vicious voice. The disgusting voice of my nemesis spoke up saying, **"THIS IS NOT THE END"**. I have a feeling he wanted to say something more but unfortunately our oh-so-magical school collapsed on us.

IDEA BANK - Draw, paint, doodle or write what you liked/disliked in this book. Leave notes for your friends or simply finish that maths sum you have been avoiding

...but, is it?

...But is it the End Yet?

The end is just a new beginning.

– J. Stanford

No school seems like dream right? Trust me school ON you is a bigger nightmare than you IN school. That snake ruined all my plans for a midnight feast+ almost killed my teachers and friends. Duryodhana Sir's mace created a weird magnetic field and attracted all the heavier pieces of rubble and stone towards it (yes, a mace was more useful than all of us combined). The children were immediately hospitalised and Dr.S tended to us personally. Manthara and Shakuni told stories about war criminals, war wounds and war deaths that made us grateful for what we had left. The makeshift hospital was pretty modernised and Ranvir and Ragini were also counselled and had to attend therapy sessions with wait for it....Surpanakha (don't even ask me why her). It was not a typical happy ending but everyone was alive which was more than I could expect.

Everyone took turns telling me, vomit girl (yes, that is unofficially my superhero name). Where had that snaky being gone? No clue. But all ends that ends well. Or so I believed before…

THE END

(JUST KIDDING!)

GLOSSARY

- Ravan/Mr.Avran: The quintessential villain of "Ram-Rajya" or the perfect kingdom. The hero was exiled, his (Ravan's) sister fell in love with the hero, hero's brother cut her nose, Ravan kidnapped hero's wife…big, bad war. The usual.
- Duryodhana/Mr. Dyourdhana: His family played the first game of family feud. Cousins fighting for a throne…odds are a 100:5…guess who won? (The five brothers won).
- Daksh/Mr. Shakad: That overprotective father whose daughter no one wants to date? Yes, that is him. He was the reason for his daughter's death and his son-in-law's dangerous dance.
- Holika/Miss Kaholi: Tried to burn her nephew on her brother's advice. Had the strongest brother-sister bond. I said *'tried to'*, obviously she failed.
- Manthara/Miss Rathmana: Ultimate gossip girl… bad mouthed about the queen's stepson to the queen. Let's just say it ended badly for everyone.
- Kaikeyi/Mrs.Keikaiy: The queen whose stepson Manthara bad-mouthed about. Wanted to make her

son the king. Forced her stepson out of the kingdom starting a rather unfortunate chain of events (for details: see Ravan and Manthara's description).

- Surpanakha/Miss.Sukarphana: First girl *"jisne apni naak kaathwa di"*. She basically tried to act lovey-dovey to a married man and his brother (who was also married) and went a little homicidal when no one agreed and tried to kill the former's wife which resulted in her nose getting cut. Cried to her brother about it who solved the matter maturely by starting a war (yes, before you ask, said brother is Ravan).

- Shakuni/Mr.Akushin: This guy was plain genius. He played a better game of chess than Ron (some major reference). He taught his nephew to play the awesome game of chess which led to his winning a palace, a kingdom and the wife of the opponent (last one was thankfully returned).

- Kansa/Mr.Sanak: Two power hungry uncles are in a row...Shakuni might have bagged the 'Best Uncle of the year' trophy but Kansa is no less...Kansa killed 8...you read it right EIGHT of his sister's kids as ONE of her kids was supposed to kill him. As fate would have it, the ninth kid survived.

- Karnabhakum/Mr.Kumbhakarna: Slept for six months and ate for the rest (when awake of course), wiped out majority of the opponent's army. Moral of the story: Hibernation and over-eating are the ways to win a war (terms and conditions apply*... you have to be super strong and a giant in short).

- Vissy: A completely FICTIONAL *ahem*ahem* monster who is the best, most manipulative and the coolest villain.
- Metamorphosis: A school with Sanskrit swag and awesome-ness, also one which believes in second chances.

NOTE: This book is written on paper (duh). We get paper from trees. Trees give us oxygen. All these facts lead to one conclusion, WE MUST SAVE TREES. So please, as a request, plant a tree...plant one, two... plant a hundred. If not for yourself or for the environment, then for the generations of humans who may not be able to read, write or even breathe as we couldn't take out the time and plant one tree. I cannot force you, nor can anyone else. Only your conscience can do that. So if you are reading it (even in an eBook format) I would strongly suggest that you plant a tree. Thousands of trees have been cut but not one replanted and so I humbly request you dear reader to do your part for the environment. It is a saying that a tree smiles every time we read knowing there is life after death. We, the humans, should give back to the wonderful plants and Mother Earth by making her green again. I am not being preach-y but being realistic, if you want to breathe pure oxygen-here is your chance! If you have read / seen the book/movie the Lorax by Dr. Seuss you would know-"Unless someone like you cares an awful lot, nothing is going to get better. It's not!"

PERSONALITY TEST

What are your hobbies?

A) TAKING REVENGE FOR YOUR SISTER
B) FIGHTING WITH A SIBLING
C) GOSSIPING AND BAD MOUTHING
D) MANIPULATING PEOPLE INTO Decisions AND DAY DREAMING
E) CHANGING FORMS AND GETTING YOUR NOSE CUT
F) SLEEPING THROUGHOUT THE DAY
G) PLOTTING YOUR NEPHEW'S DEATH
H) TRYING AND FAILING TO KILL YOUR NEPHEW
I) BELITTLING YOUR SON-IN-LAW
J) PLAYING MUSIC AND PETTING HOSTILE SWANS
K) TEACHING YOUR NEPHEW HOW TO PLAY DICE
L) HAVE AN UNHEALTHY OBSESSION WITH BOOKS AND PIZZA

ANSWERS:

A) **RAVAN,**
B) **DURYODHANA,**
C) **MANTHARA,**
D) **KAIKEYI,**
E) **SURPANAKHA,**
F) **KUMBHAKARNA,**
G) **KANSA,**
H) **HOLIKA,**
I) **DAKSH,**
J) **SARASWATI,**
K) **SHAKUNI,**
L) **ME!**

Printed in the United States
By Bookmasters